BEAST QUEST

THE DARK REALM

→ BOOK SIXTEEN ←

KAYMON
THE GORGON HOUND

BEAST QUEST

THE DARK REALM

→ BOOK SIXTEEN ←

KAYMON
THE GORGON HOUND

ADAM BLADE

ILLUSTRATED BY EZRA TUCKER

SCHOLASTIC INC.

New York Toronto London Auckland
Sydney Mexico City New Delhi Hong Kong

With special thanks to Allan Frewin Jones

For Harvey

No part of this work may be reproduced, stored in a retrieval system, or transmitted in any form or by any means, electronic, mechanical, photocopying, recording, or otherwise, without written permission of the publisher. For information regarding permission, write to Working Partners Ltd., Stanley House, St Chad's Place, London WC1X 9HH, United Kingdom.

ISBN 978-0-545-20034-9

Beast Quest series created by Working Partners Ltd., London.
BEAST QUEST is a trademark of Beast Quest Ltd.

Published by Scholastic Inc., 557 Broadway, New York, NY 10012, by arrangement with Working Partners Ltd.
SCHOLASTIC, LITTLE APPLE, and associated logos are trademarks and/or registered trademarks of Scholastic Inc.

12 11 10 9 8 7 6 5 4 3 2 1   10 11 12 13 14 15/0

Designed by Tim Hall
Printed in the U.S.A.
First printing, July 2010

40

BEAST QUEST

THE DARK REALM

Welcome. You stand on the edge of darkness, at the gates of an awful land. This place is Gorgonia, the Dark Realm, where the sky is red, the water black, and Malvel rules. Tom and Elenna — your hero and his companion — must travel here to complete the next Beast Quest.

Gorgonia is home to six most deadly Beasts — Minotaur, Winged Stallion, Sea Monster, Gorgonian Hound, Mighty Mammoth, and Scorpion Man. Nothing can prepare Tom and Elenna for what they are about to face. Their past victories mean little. Only strong hearts and determination will save them now.

Dare you follow Tom's path once more? I advise you to turn back. Heroes can be stubborn and adventures may beckon, but if you decide to stay with Tom, you must be brave and fearless. Anything less will mean certain doom.

Watch your step. . . .

Kerlo the Gatekeeper

THE NIGHT WAS DARK AS THE INJURED REBEL limped away from the castle on the moor. He had used a smuggled metal file to saw through his shackles, and the jagged-toothed edge had slipped and cut into his skin. The pain in his ankle burned, but he was desperate to get away from that terrible place.

He thought of his fellow rebels languishing in the castle dungeons. Many of them had planned to escape with him, but it seemed he had been the only one to make it over the drawbridge. He threw himself under a gorse bush, gasping for breath.

"I need to rest," he muttered to himself.

After a while he crawled out and cautiously lifted his head. He frowned. A thick gray fog was sweeping across the moor like a ghostly tide, drowning the hills and valleys. The fog would make it harder for the soldiers to find him. But it would also make it difficult for him to see the prearranged signal lights of the rebels' friends.

The man stood up, staring into the blinding fog.

Where were the lights?

Wait!

He narrowed his eyes, peering into the distance. Then his heart leaped. He could see two lights, yellow dots, blurred by the fog. The signal!

He stumbled forward on his bleeding feet. Rescue was near. The lights were growing larger now, as if the bearers of lanterns were moving toward him. Two men, he assumed, walking side by side.

"Freedom or death!" he called. It was the agreed password.

He paused, listening for the response. But all

he heard was a low moan that echoed through the fog.

He shivered and frowned again. He yelled the password once more.

Now the two lights were moving swiftly toward him. But although they rose and fell in a curious loping manner, they always kept exactly the same distance apart. Then a second low moan rumbled through the fog, and this time there was another noise — the unmistakable sound of large teeth snapping.

Suddenly, something huge came hurtling toward him out of the fog. The man let out a cry, throwing up his arms to protect his face. Through his fingers, he saw the salivating fangs of an enormous hound. The lights he'd seen were the Beast's ferocious yellow eyes!

A moment later, the snarling creature was upon him, throwing him onto his back, its savage claws ripping at his chest and face. . . .

CHAPTER ONE

DEADLY FLOWERS

TOM AND ELENNA STOOD IN THE BOW OF THEIR boat as they returned to the shore of the Black Ocean. With the defeat of Narga the Sea Monster, another good Beast of Avantia had been freed — Sepron the Sea Serpent. The two friends leaped down onto the beach, eager to be reunited with their animal companions. Silver the wolf let out a howl of delight, and Storm, Tom's black stallion, reared, neighing triumphantly.

Tom and Elenna already knew that another Quest lay ahead. Wizard Aduro, their friend and mentor, had briefly appeared on the ocean waves, warning them that they would soon face another evil Beast: Kaymon. But he hadn't given them any more details.

Tom touched the blue sapphire from Narga's tooth, which he had won in the last fight. He had placed it in his magic belt next to the ruby, which gave him the ability to understand the good Beasts, and the emerald with its power to heal broken bones. This new jewel gave him a knife-sharp memory. When he touched it, he remembered all the battles he had won in his Quest to rid Avantia of the Dark Wizard Malvel.

"Tom, look!" said Elenna.

Tom turned and saw that his companion was looking at the greasy, foul-smelling map of Gorgonia that Malvel had given them. She was pointing to a tiny picture of Tartok the Ice Beast that had appeared on the map.

Tom felt a sharp tingling in his shield. Tartok's claw, embedded there with the tokens of the other five good Beasts, was quivering.

Tom looked back at the map and the little image of Tartok. "Don't worry, my friend," he said. "We'll save you!"

"It looks as though she's being held captive somewhere in the south of Gorgonia," Elenna said. "But what kind of Beast could take her prisoner? She's one of the strongest of the good Beasts."

"Aduro said Kaymon was more evil than we could possibly imagine," Tom warned her.

"But what can that mean?" Elenna wondered aloud.

"I think it's time we found out," Tom replied. The thought of Tartok being held prisoner burned his heart. "Come on, Storm — we have work to do!"

He leaped into the saddle and extended an arm to help Elenna up behind him.

"To the south!" Tom cried. "Let's rescue Tartok!"

The noble stallion galloped beneath the seething red Gorgonian skies, Silver at his side. Tom shivered, looking up at the red clouds that rolled and swirled above their heads. He would never get used to this terrible land!

"Don't forget to avoid the quicksand we wandered into before," Elenna said.

Tom nodded. "I remember it perfectly," he told her. "In fact, I can remember every hill and valley of this part of Gorgonia, thanks to Narga's sapphire."

"That's good," Elenna said. "Especially since we can't completely trust Malvel's map. Remember the trouble it got us into last time?"

Soon the Black Ocean was far behind them and the sun was low on the horizon. They entered a grim landscape of broken hills.

"Have you noticed it's getting much hotter?" Tom said, wiping sweat from his forehead. "It must be terrible for Tartok to be imprisoned here." The ice beast was used to Avantia's northern ice fields, her thick black fur protecting her from bitter winter winds.

As they reached the top of the first hill, they found themselves staring into a wide valley filled with bluebells.

"Oh, how beautiful!" Elenna said. "I would never have expected to find such lovely flowers in a place like this." She frowned. "But what's that shape in the middle? I can't make it out."

Tom peered across the valley. Although the precious suit of golden armor had been returned to Avantia, he still possessed its powers, and the armor's helmet allowed him to see far into the distance.

"It's Tartok!" he said. "The poor Beast is chained to a rock!"

Shackled to a huge rock of amber, Tartok still looked majestic, her thick dark fur glowing under the red clouds. But she was wrenching and tearing at the chain, clearly in great distress.

"That's so cruel!" cried Elenna. "How could anyone cause her so much pain?" She sprang down

• **9** •

from the saddle and began to run down the hillside. Silver ran beside her as she headed toward the blue sea of flowers.

"Be careful!" Tom called, urging Storm down the hillside after them. He wasn't at all sure about those bluebells, which had turned toward Elenna, almost as if they knew she was approaching.

"Wait!" Tom shouted, as Elenna and Silver waded into the waist-high flowers.

A moment later Elenna stopped and began beating at the flowers with her hands.

"Tom! Help!" she shouted.

At her side, Silver was leaping back and forth, howling and snarling as though he were being attacked by an invisible enemy.

Tom could see what was happening. The dark red stamens of the flowers were stabbing like tiny daggers, hemming Elenna and Silver in with their needle-sharp blades.

Silver was yelping in pain.

"Ouch!" Elenna cried. "Tom — it's so painful."

Tom pulled on his reins and brought Storm to a halt. He swung down from the saddle. There was only one thing he could do. Gripping his shield, Tom drew his sword and swung his blade through the vicious flowers, cutting a path toward his friends.

The flowers stabbed at him as he raced through. He felt pain as sharp as wasp stings as he sliced through the stems. Using the speed given to him by the golden leg armor, he quickly reached Elenna and the wolf.

"Come on!" Tom called, alarmed to see that the bluebells were swarming behind him, lunging forward to fill the gap that he had made.

Elenna and Silver raced along with Tom close behind. The flowers writhed all around them, lunging at them like snakes. At last they came diving out of the flowers, skidding in the dust as they reached safety.

Tom stared out over the bluebells. Tartok was still in the center of the flowers, looking toward him in desperation. She lifted her arms and rattled her chain in anguish.

"The evil flowers are all around her," Tom said. "How will we ever be able to reach her?"

Then a low, mournful howl came echoing across the valley.

Tom and Elenna looked at each other.

"What was that?" Elenna asked.

Tom gripped his sword firmly. "Kaymon!" he said.

→ CHAPTER TWO ←

KAYMON'S POWER

THE EERIE HOWL RANG OUT AGAIN.

"It sounds so lonely," Elenna murmured, her voice trembling.

"But it sounds evil, too," Tom said, as a third howl drifted on the wind. "Look!" He pointed to a dark shape on the hilltops to the west, silhouetted against the bloodred disk of the setting sun. With his extrakeen vision, Tom could see terrible yellow eyes that shone with a wicked light.

"It's a hound, Elenna!" he said.

A moment later, Kaymon came leaping down from the hilltop, still some distance away but hurtling rapidly toward them with gnashing,

slobbering fangs. Soon she was crashing through the blue flowers. Her teeth ripped the heads off the flowers, and her huge feet crushed them as she tore a path toward Tom and his companions.

Storm tossed his head, his eyes rolling, as the hound drew rapidly closer. The fur bristled all along Silver's grizzled back and he bayed, pawing the ground.

Kaymon was as large as a bull and her thick black fur was tangled and caked with filth. And there was a smell, too — a foul, choking stench that made Tom reel.

As the Beast pounded forward, Tom saw the evil light in her eyes and the terrible strength of her shoulders and flanks. He also noticed something else — the Beast wore a thick collar of twisted gold around her neck, and set deep into the precious metal was a huge white diamond.

Tom caught hold of Storm's reins and stepped in front of Elenna, drawing his sword.

"Keep back!" he said to his friends. He waited, sword in hand, as the hound came crashing out of the flowers.

Suddenly, Silver jumped past him, his teeth bared as he sprang at the Beast's throat.

"Silver, no!" Tom shouted.

But the wolf ignored his cries. Leaping high with his jaws wide, he sank his teeth into Kaymon's neck.

The hound snarled and howled, shaking her head as she tried to free herself. But Silver's jaws held her in a deadly grip, his claws ripping at the Beast's fur.

For a few moments Silver put up a tremendous fight. But then Kaymon let out a ferocious roar and her whole body suddenly began to swell, writhing and distorting and changing shape so that Silver lost his grip and was thrown off.

"What's happening?" Elenna cried.

"She's changing!" Tom shouted in horror.

Instead of one hound, there were now three!

Tom stared in disbelief, his heart almost stopping in his chest.

Each of the Beasts was as huge and as savage as the first, and all three turned on Silver as he stood panting and snarling.

"He doesn't stand a chance!" Elenna cried as the hounds leaped on the startled wolf.

Silver vanished from sight under the dark bulk of their powerful bodies, his angry growls drowned out by the snapping and snarling of the three hounds.

Tom turned to Elenna. "Take Storm's reins," he said urgently. "I have to rescue Silver!" He tightened his grip on his shield and brandished his sword as he ran forward.

One of the hounds turned from the wolf, her yellow eyes blazing. A moment later and she was in the air, leaping at Tom's head.

"Watch out!" he heard Elenna shout.

Tom lifted his shield to deflect the sharp claws that were reaching out to gouge his eyes. The weight of the hound sent him staggering backward and he almost fell, but he managed to hold his ground, digging in his heels. Using the strength given to him by the golden breastplate, he used his shield to block the hound's charge and send her crashing to one side. Then, with a sharp twist of his wrist, his sword pierced the hound's thick fur. Dark blood spurted from the wound as the hound yelped in pain and turned tail, running away into the dusk.

Tom saw a second hound racing toward Elenna and Storm. Swift as lightning, Elenna fitted an arrow to her bow and let it fly. She shot three arrows, one after another, into the Beast as she hurtled toward Elenna. The third arrow embedded itself deep into the hound's leg. Howling wildly, the evil creature twisted around, trying to bite at it.

"Well done!" Tom shouted, running toward his friends. The wounded Beast came to a tumbling halt; then she, too, raced away, snarling with pain. They had beaten two of the evil Beasts!

But the third hound was standing over Silver. The wolf was lying on the ground, dreadfully still. Tom's heart was in his throat. Was Silver already dead?

"No!" Tom yelled, running swiftly toward the third hound, his sword flashing.

Kaymon turned, her jaws opening and her eyes burning with ferocious evil.

For a moment Tom and the evil Beast looked into each other's eyes.

Then Tom raised his sword, aiming to plunge it into the monster's chest. But the hound turned and raced away through the sea of flowers, following the other two fleeing Beasts toward the distant hills.

"Come back and fight!" Tom shouted after

them. He ran into the bluebells, beating the darting stamens back with his shield, determined to follow the escaping Beast.

But a whimper from Silver stopped him. He paused, looking over his shoulder to where the wolf lay on the ground. Elenna knelt at Silver's side, cradling the wolf's head in her lap. Storm stood over them, whinnying anxiously.

Silver was badly injured, his flesh torn open all along his neck and flanks, his fur matted and blood-soaked from the claws and fangs of the three evil hounds.

"I can't leave Silver like this!" Tom murmured. But before going to the wolf, he lifted his sword and shouted, "No matter how far you run, Kaymon, we will meet again. I promise!"

CHAPTER THREE

THE BINDING CHAIN

SILVER LAY PANTING WITH QUICK, SHALLOW breaths, his eyes rolling back and his tongue lolling. Tom shuddered at the sight of the wolf's bloody wounds. Some of his ribs looked broken.

Elenna wept, gently stroking Silver's neck, her tears mingling with the blood on his fur. "Can you save him, Tom?"

"I still have Epos's healing token, as well as the emerald," Tom told her. "I'm sure they'll be powerful enough to make Silver well again."

Tom hoped he sounded more confident than he felt. The healing token and the emerald had only previously been used on himself and on the good

Beasts — he had no way of knowing if they would work on Silver.

He knelt at the wolf's side, taking the flame bird's feather from his shield and the emerald from his belt. He touched them against the worst of Silver's wounds — a hideous gash on his side — and the broken ribs.

Tom felt a sudden surge of energy, and pulses of red and green light flashed through his fingers as the healing power of the two tokens began to work together.

"His ribs are mending," Tom whispered. "Look!"

The arc of Silver's ribs was returning and the wounds were closing, the blood around them disappearing.

"Yes, I can see!" Elenna gasped, wiping the tears from her eyes. "Tom — that's wonderful!"

The energy sent a tingling power up Tom's arm as he watched the broken ribs knit together under the flesh. In a few more moments the gray fur was thick again over the healed wounds. But the poor wolf was still weak and exhausted from his ordeal.

Tom stood up, staring out across the sea of blue flowers to where Tartok was still held captive, chained to the amber rock. The light was fading rapidly now, the amber glowing in the dusk. Now that Silver was better, it was time for Tom to act! There was no time to waste.

He took several steps back. Gathering all his strength, he ran and, at the very edge of the bluebells, leaped up into air, harnessing the power of the golden boots, as the flowers snapped at his heels.

"Oh, *yes*!" he shouted in excitement as he soared through the air, stretching out his legs for the landing. He knew it was going to be close. . . .

But even such a great leap was not enough to clear the flowers. He landed near Tartok's clearing, but right among the deadly blooms. The red stamens stabbed at him. Using his shield to ward

them off, he strode toward the ice beast, hacking at the bluebells with his sword.

Tartok roared and surged forward to greet him, her long, shaggy arms open. Tom sensed the good Beast's joy and relief as he stepped into the clearing. But the chain jerked her back, and her face crumpled with pain and anger as she tugged at the heavy iron links that held her captive to the amber rock.

"I'll set you free!" Tom promised. He could see great sores where the chain had been rubbing his friend's skin.

Tartok grunted and snorted as Tom inspected the shackles. Each link was as thick as his wrist, and the heavy chain was attached to the rock by great iron staples, driven deep into the amber.

"I'm going to cut the chain with my sword," Tom told the ice beast. He picked up a length of chain and hung it over part of the amber rock. Taking a deep breath, he stepped back. He lifted his sword above his head in both hands and brought it crashing down onto the iron links. Clang! Tom's arms shivered to the shoulder with the impact. But the chain held.

He could faintly hear Elenna shouting, "Come on, Tom! You can do it!"

Gritting his teeth, Tom lifted his sword again.

He brought the sword down with all his might. There was an echoing crack and a glow of amber light; then the chain broke apart!

Tartok rose up onto her back legs and gave a roar of delight while Tom held his sword above his head in triumph.

Now they needed to get back to where Elenna and the others were waiting. Tom couldn't just jump across the flowers and leave Tartok behind. They had to do this together. He started hacking at the flowers, to cut a path through to his companions.

Then Tartok scooped Tom up in her great arms

and perched him high on her shoulder. He clung to her fur as she began to make her way through the flowers.

"Thanks, Tartok!" he said, laughing.

The blue heads turned and the stamens stabbed viciously, but Tartok's fur was too thick for their evil blades. She plowed onward, crushing the flowers beneath her huge feet. At last they made it through the sea of flowers and were reunited with Tom's friends.

Tartok was free!

But Tom knew that was not enough.

"Kaymon is still out there," he said. "Our next task is to find her and defeat her so we can send Tartok home." He looked at Elenna. "I will not let Malvel win!"

The Quest was far from over.

CHAPTER FOUR

THE BEAST ON THE BATTLEMENTS

NIGHT HAD FALLEN, AND THE GORGONIAN SKY was gloomy and starless.

"We *will* find a way to get you back to Avantia," Tom vowed to Tartok. "But Elenna and I need to find Kaymon first." He hoped the ice beast would understand what he was asking of her, and concentrated on the ruby in his belt, knowing it would help him to communicate. "Will you stay here and protect Silver and Storm while we are gone?"

The good Beast frowned; then a gleam of understanding came into her eyes and she grunted and nodded, one large hand reaching out to rest on Storm's neck, the other gently stroking Silver's fur as he lay beside her.

"Why do you want to leave them all behind?" Elenna asked in a soft voice.

"There are three hounds out there," Tom said. "We won't be able to concentrate on defeating Kaymon if she can attack our friends when we're distracted. We need to focus all her attention on *us*."

Elenna looked uneasily at him. "I don't know, Tom," she murmured. "Will the two of us be enough?"

"Don't forget," said Tom, "that we also have the powers from the magic shield and the golden armor." He put his hand on Elenna's shoulder. "We can do this," he said. "While there is blood in my veins, I will end this Quest!"

An excited light sparked in Elenna's eyes. "So will I!" she said.

Tom looked up into the bleak night sky. "We should sleep now," he said. "We can take turns to keep watch for Kaymon. And then, at first light, the Quest continues!"

As the red sun rose over the hills the next morning, Tom was already on his feet. Elenna took a few moments to bid farewell to Silver. The wolf was still very weak, but he licked Elenna's face gratefully.

"Are you sure you want to leave him?" Tom asked. "I can do this alone, if I need to."

"No!" Elenna said fiercely. "Kaymon hurt Silver. I'm going with you to find her!"

Tom said good-bye to Tartok and the animals, and the two friends headed off in pursuit of the Gorgon hound.

"We can circle the bluebells and pick up Kaymon's trail on the far side of the valley," Tom said.

There they saw three sets of large paw marks that led up the hillside and across the rugged countryside. The hills were jagged and sharp-edged, like rows of broken teeth. A few bare plants grew among the rocks, every twig armed with a razor-sharp thorn.

After a while Tom noticed that the three sets of markings were becoming closer together. Suddenly, they merged into a single, much heavier trail.

"The hounds joined together again here," Tom said. "Kaymon must split into three only when she's in danger."

Soon Tom and Elenna crested a hill and found themselves staring at a dark castle standing on a mound in the middle of a bleak moor.

Elenna opened the map. "There's no castle shown here," she said.

Tom stared out across the moor, his keen vision bringing the gloomy fortress into sharp focus. It was surrounded by a moat of murky green water. Tom narrowed his eyes. The towering granite walls looked as though they contained dreadful secrets.

"I don't like the look of it," Elenna said with a shudder.

Tom's eyes rose to the jagged battlements. Something was moving up there.

"I see Kaymon!" he said.

Pacing back and forth, high on the battlements, her tail swinging, was the great hound. Then she stopped pacing, and turned toward Tom and Elenna, her yellow eyes burning. A moment later, the wide jaws opened and a terrible howl echoed out across the moor.

"She's seen us," Elenna said.

Tom drew his sword. "Then we shouldn't keep her waiting!" he said.

CHAPTER FIVE

THE EVIL CASTLE

Tom and Elenna ran through the long grass of the moor, zigzagging as they approached the castle. They darted between mounds and low hills, hoping that Kaymon would lose sight of them. Finally, they arrived at a ditch, where they lay to catch their breath. They were halfway to the castle now. It towered up, pitch-black against the swirling red sky.

"The drawbridge is down," Tom said to Elenna, as he peered out of the ditch. "And the gate is open. There's no sign of any people and there aren't any lights. Perhaps the castle is abandoned?"

"We can't be sure of that," Elenna said.

"I know," Tom replied. He felt uneasy. "But we have to go in there."

"Can you see Kaymon?" Elenna asked.

"No. Not from here." Tom summoned his courage. "Come on."

They raced toward the castle, crouching low, and began to cross the drawbridge. The wooden boards groaned underneath them, and as Tom came to the middle, the rotting timbers cracked under his foot. He drew back as a piece of wood fell down into the stinking, weed-choked waters of the moat, leaving a ragged hole.

"Be careful," he said to Elenna. "The drawbridge is falling to pieces!"

They moved forward, testing each step before putting their weight on the decayed wooden boards.

Tom looked around as they entered the gateway. The stones were slimy. Foul-smelling water oozed and dripped all around them. They stepped into a courtyard. The castle was totally silent. Doors hung open on their hinges, revealing glimpses of rooms where the furniture was overturned as though people had left in a panic.

"What do you think happened here?" Elenna asked, looking anxiously around. "Where is everyone?"

"Perhaps Kaymon chased them away," Tom suggested. He looked up toward the battlements. There was no sign of the evil Beast.

"Where is she?" Elenna asked.

"That's what I want to know," Tom said. "We have to find her before she finds us!" He held his sword out in front of him as he moved around the courtyard, kicking doors open as he searched for the Beast.

"Keep back," he warned Elenna. "But keep an arrow on the string and be ready to fire the moment the Beast appears."

They made their way into one of the rooms.

Open doors led into more rooms, but still they found nothing.

"Perhaps she's gone?" Elenna murmured.

"I doubt it," Tom replied. "She's ready for a fight."

The faintest of sounds came up from beneath the floorboards.

"Was that a voice?" Elenna asked, her eyes wide.

Tom took a deep breath. "Hello!" he shouted. "Is anyone there?"

They strained their ears, hardly breathing. The sound came again, and this time there was no doubt — human voices were echoing up from deep beneath their feet.

At the same moment, a deep-throated howl boomed through the castle. Tom frowned, striding out into the courtyard. High on the battlements above the gatehouse, he saw Kaymon pacing slowly along the wall. Tom's fingers closed around the hilt of his sword.

Then he noticed a movement in the shadows. A tall, bald-headed man emerged into the light. His clothes were ragged and he held a staff of gnarled wood. A patch covered one eye.

"Kerlo!" Tom gasped, recognizing the gatekeeper who had greeted him when he had first entered Gorgonia.

The man leaned on his staff, watching Tom keenly with his one eye. "It sounds as though someone needs help," he commented.

Elenna appeared at the doorway. She looked at the gatekeeper for a moment, then turned to Tom. "The voices are getting louder," she called. "They sound desperate."

Tom stared up at Kaymon, who was still pacing. Then he drew his sword and followed Elenna inside. He would tackle the hound later. First he had to rescue the captives trapped in the castle's dark heart.

CHAPTER SIX

THE DUNGEONS

TOM AND ELENNA RAN, LOOKING FOR A WAY into the lower regions of the castle.

They pushed through a creaking door and came into a long corridor with dank walls lit by flaming torches.

"What was Kerlo doing here?" Elenna asked. "I feel as if he's on our side, although I can never be sure."

"I know what you mean," Tom replied. "I don't always understand what he says, but I'm almost certain he's not our enemy."

They passed several doorways, but these led only to other deserted rooms. Winding stairways brought them deep under the ground where the air was stale and musty. Rats scuttled away.

"This place is huge," Elenna said. "How will we ever find the captives?"

"We must!" Tom insisted. "Let's listen!"

They stood in a cobwebbed stone corridor, holding their breath, and heard the clamor of trapped people beneath them.

A single voice rose above the others. "Help us! Please help us!"

Tom stared at a ragged tapestry that hung on the wall. Its threadbare edge twitched as if disturbed by a breath of wind.

Tom strode over and pulled aside the tapestry, revealing an arched doorway. It led to another stone stairway that wound into the depths, its walls lit by smoking torches. He looked at Elenna. "This is the way!" He took a torch from the wall and together they made their way down into the gloom of the castle's deepest cellars.

Tom shuddered at the sight of the grimy, stinking dungeons. Water trickled down the walls, and patches of fungus clung to the stones, glowing with a sickly light. Clumps of sticky spiderwebs stuck to their clothing as they brushed past.

"This is terrible," Elenna whispered, her voice full of dread.

The voices grew louder. "We're here! Help us!"

Tom turned a corner and at last he saw the prisoners. There were about a dozen men in a filthy chamber, their limbs shackled in rusting chains, their clothes in tatters.

The prisoners pulled against their chains. "Help us! Free us!" they called out.

Tom and Elenna ran forward, taking out their drinking flasks and giving the men a drink.

"Who are you?" Tom asked.

One man, taller and broader than the others, got to his feet, his chains rattling in the iron ring that held them to the wall.

"We are Gorgonian rebels," he said. "Have you come over the moor? Did you see any of our comrades out there?"

Tom shook his head. "I'm sorry," he said. "I didn't see anyone."

"Please free us," the man said.

Tom looked at the shackles. The iron was rusted and old. "Keep still!" he warned the man, taking out his sword and thrusting the tip into the locking mechanism. He gave his sword a sharp twist. The blade slipped and grazed the man's skin. He hissed with the pain.

"I'm sorry," Tom gasped. "I'll try that again."

He really needed to concentrate!

He pressed the tip of his sword to the shackles a second time. The man watched him anxiously. He twisted the blade again and this time the iron cuff snapped open.

"Thank you," the man said. "Free my men and we will be gone from here."

It wasn't long before all the rebels had been released from their chains. They stood up, rubbing their numbed limbs, smiling with gratitude and relief.

"Who are you?" the tall man asked, resting his hand on Tom's shoulder and looking sharply at Elenna.

"We come from another land," Tom said. "We're friends of a good wizard." He wasn't sure how much he should tell these people.

"You have aided the rebellion!" the man said. "Thank you! But tell no one that you ever saw us. Malvel must not get to hear of this!"

Tom shivered at the mention of the evil wizard's name. "Malvel will hear nothing from us," he said. "Can we do anything else to help?" He felt sure that anyone rebelling against Malvel had to be good.

"You have done enough," the man said. "But remember: Never speak of this encounter!" He led his men out of the dungeon and soon they were gone.

The gatekeeper stepped suddenly from the shadows.

"Was that wise?" Kerlo asked, his one keen eye on Tom's face.

Tom stared at him, troubled by a moment of doubt.

"They were starving," Elenna said. "We had to let them go."

Kerlo's piercing eye turned to her. "Did you, indeed?" he growled. "Do you know what acts these men are capable of?"

Tom looked at the gatekeeper, uncertainty creeping into his mind. Had they been right to set those men free? "They are against Malvel. They're on the same side as us — aren't they?" he asked.

But Kerlo just turned and walked slowly up the stairway without replying.

Tom was about to mount the stairs after him when the flickering light of his torch shone on something that had been crammed into a crevice in the entrance to the stairway.

He moved the torch closer. It was a folded scrap of linen. He pulled it free. Elenna leaned over his shoulder as he carefully opened it.

"What is that?" Elenna asked.

"It's a lock of hair," Tom said in surprise. "And a piece of red silk."

Elenna let out a gasp. She picked up the lock of chestnut hair and held it against Tom's head. "It's exactly the same color as yours!" she whispered.

Bewildered, Tom picked up the scrap of scarlet silk. "There's something embroidered on it," he murmured. "Elenna — hold it for me so I can shine the light on it."

Elenna stretched the silk between her fingers.

It was a curling script, sewn onto the silk with

fine yellow thread. "'Midsummer's Eve,'" Tom read. "But . . . but that's my birthday!"

The two friends looked at each other.

"Could it have been left here by your lost father?" Elenna asked.

Tom had never seen his father, Taladon, who had disappeared when Tom was a baby.

"Do you think he may have been here?" his friend continued.

Tom stared again at the piece of silk. To think that his father might have stood in this very spot! For a moment, he felt closer to Taladon than he ever had before. His hand closed around the scrap.

"Come on, Elenna," he said. "Taladon would want me to do the right thing. We have an evil Beast to defeat."

Tom raced up the stone stairs. He was ready to bring this Quest to an end!

⇥ CHAPTER SEVEN ⇤

DEFEAT!

A DEEP-THROATED HOWL ECHOED DOWN THE stairwell.

"Kaymon!" gasped Elenna. "She sounds close!"

"She must have come down from the battlements!" Tom said, pushing the linen rag and the scrap of red silk into his tunic.

He raced up the stairs, groping in his pocket for his magical compass, which his father had left him. The scrap of silk had reminded him of it. The needle could point to Danger or Destiny to help Tom make vital decisions. He took it out as he ran along the corridor and saw that the needle was wavering.

There was no sign of the rebels. Tom guessed that they must have left the castle.

He heard Elenna right behind him as he came back into the room that led to the courtyard. Beyond the open door, he could see the huge shape of Kaymon moving restlessly to and fro, waiting for Tom.

Tom looked at the compass again. Now the needle rested firmly over the word Destiny.

Pocketing the compass, Tom drew his sword. Its blade reflected the red sky, flashing like a tongue of fire as he approached the courtyard. He lifted his shield, his muscles flexing as he prepared to do battle. Then he stepped out into the open, his boots ringing on the cobbles. Elenna was at his shoulder, an arrow poised on her bow, her eyes gleaming.

"Keep me covered," Tom said to Elenna. "But don't put yourself in danger."

He moved into the center of the courtyard,

keeping his eyes fixed on the prowling Beast. Kaymon paced back and forth, her feet thumping and her claws rattling on the stones. The evil Beast's yellow eyes were filled with malice.

Lifting his sword, Tom closed in.

Kaymon paused, her throat rumbling with a low, menacing growl.

"This is for Silver!" Tom shouted as he rushed toward the Beast.

Kaymon crouched low, growling as Tom came at her. Then she flexed her mighty leg muscles and leaped right over Tom's head! Tom thrust his sword up high, slicing the air, but the Beast was out of range.

Tom turned swiftly, his shield up and his sword ready.

The Beast landed on the stone steps that led to the battlements. Howling, Kaymon leaped again, high above Tom's head. But this time, in the middle of the leap, the shape of the Beast swelled — and suddenly, there were three hounds in the air.

They separated and came crashing down onto the cobbles with a noise like an avalanche. Tom spun around. The three hounds had surrounded him, their eyes burning with sinister satisfaction as they moved slowly forward, their menacing growls filling the courtyard. Tom turned, trying desperately to keep all three Beasts at bay with his flashing sword. But as he turned to confront two of the hounds, the third leaped forward behind him, one great paw reaching out, claws gleaming.

Using the power given to him by the golden boots, Tom sprang over the hound's head. Jaws snapped at his heels as he soared through the air. He twisted in midleap, his feet striking high on the courtyard wall. He flexed his knees and kicked out, the force sending him flying across the courtyard above the howling Beasts.

"For Avantia!" he shouted, striking down at them with his sword as he sped over their heads.

"Well done!" Elenna called.

Tom felt full of energy and strength as he landed on the cobbles, the golden chain mail giving him extra strength of heart in battle. The hounds pounced, but before they were able to sink their fangs into him, he leaped high again, turning a somersault in midair.

One hound jumped up, razor-sharp claws raking and teeth gnashing. Tom stamped hard on the hound's muzzle, bounding high again and backflipping before he came plunging down to the ground.

The hounds howled with rage. Tom watched as they came for him. He intended to make another leap, hoping they would crash into one another. But he left his jump a moment too late.

One of the hounds reached out with a great paw,

and the curled yellow claws struck Tom on the wrist, knocking his sword out of his fingers. The steel blade clattered as it hit the cobbles. The hound's paw reached out again, the dreadful claws catching the sword and sending it skimming across the courtyard, out of Tom's reach.

Ignoring the pain in his wrist, Tom gripped his shield and watched the three hounds pad relentlessly toward him.

They were unstoppable!

Tom braced himself as the hounds lunged toward him, their teeth dripping saliva and their twisted claws reaching for him. Would he survive?

CHAPTER EIGHT

BRAINS AGAINST BRAWN

THE THREE HOUNDS POUNCED AS ONE. BUT Tom sprang straight up into the air, and the hounds crashed together, howling and yelping.

Tom plunged downward, landing with all his weight on the head of one of the hounds. He used the Beast's huge head as a springboard, leaping sideways this time, and cartwheeling over the hound's back.

He landed hard, skidding across the cobbles, using his shield to protect him from injury. Then he retrieved his sword and crouched with his back to the wall, ready for the next attack.

The three hounds turned to him, their eyes

brimming with hatred, their hair bristling like wire along their backs.

While there is blood in my veins, he thought, *it is my destiny to confront these evil creatures — and defeat them.*

But it was still three to one! For every set of deadly fangs Tom avoided, two more were ready to take their place.

An arrow flew from Elenna's bow. It skipped on the cobbles close to the front paw of one hound. The Beast turned, her eyes fixing on Elenna, her jaws slavering.

Tom had to stop the hounds from attacking Elenna! *I must trap them,* he thought. He dashed along the wall and bounded through an open doorway. Then he slammed the door shut, hammering home the bolt before racing across the room and leaping through another door that led into a long corridor.

Glancing back, he saw the hounds smash open

the first door. They fought and struggled to get in through the entrance. At last, they forced their way into the room, snarling and biting at one another.

Tom's plan was working. In the narrow confines of the castle, there wasn't room for three massive hounds.

Tom could see Elenna beyond the doorway. "Shoot at them!" he called. "Don't let them out into the open again! I want them to chase me!"

"It's too dangerous for you!" Elenna shouted.

"No, it isn't!" Tom yelled back. "If they want to catch me inside, they'll have to change back to single form. Then I have more chance of winning!"

Moments later, an arrow sped in through the doorway, grazing the flank of one of the hounds.

Well done, Elenna! Tom thought.

He raced along the corridor, looking over his shoulder. Driven on by Elenna's arrows, the three hounds all tried to push through the second doorway. They were snapping and growling and thrashing about as each tried to get into the corridor ahead of the others.

"Come and get me!" Tom shouted. "If you can!"

The three mouths opened wide in howls of rage and frustration, the dreadful din echoing along the corridor. Tom laughed as the creatures merged together once more. He'd done it!

A moment later, one huge Kaymon came thundering down the corridor with death in her eyes. Tom noticed that the Beast was panting heavily, her chest heaving as though her heart were pounding fit to burst. Thick saliva drooled from her fangs, and her twisted claws scratched deep grooves in the stonework as she tore forward.

Tom swept the tapestry aside and ran down into the dungeons. His heart hammering, he slipped into the shadows at the foot of the winding staircase. Howling, Kaymon came hurtling down in pursuit. As the Beast passed him, Tom dodged back up the stairs. Kaymon turned at the sound of his feet, but lost her balance and tumbled over. She got up slowly, panting hard, her chest rising and falling rapidly. She was tiring, her body too huge for all this chasing.

As Tom ran into the corridor again, he heard claws scrabbling on the stone staircase behind him. This was not going to be easy! He raced along the corridor and stumbled back into the first room.

Elenna was there, an arrow to her bow.

"Keep out of sight," Tom gasped as he ran past her. "Let her pass you. Shoot at her from behind if she looks like she's giving chase. She's tiring. I think her heart could give out!"

"Good luck!" Elenna said.

Tom headed out into the courtyard and made for the steps that led to the battlements.

As Tom arrived at the top of the battlements, he

saw Kaymon at the foot of the steps. The great Beast was clearly in trouble — her mouth hanging open and her red tongue lolling. There were flecks of foam at her lips.

"Come on!" Tom taunted. "Don't give up now!"

Kaymon let out a howl that made the stones under Tom's feet tremble. Gathering all her remaining strength, the Beast mounted the stairs in three leaps. Tom ran as fast as he could. Elenna was down in the courtyard, firing arrows that skipped on the stones, narrowly missing the gasping Beast as she came careering along the battlements toward Tom.

Tom raced to the gatehouse and leaped onto it. He stared down at the drawbridge that spanned the weed-choked moat and looked back over his shoulder — Kaymon was still chasing him, her chest heaving and her breath ragged. Tom jumped from the battlements. He knew that the token of

Cypher the Mountain Giant, a tear from the Beast embedded in his shield, would protect him from the fall.

He could hear Elenna shouting encouragement from the courtyard as he dropped through the air.

He came thudding down on the rotting timbers of the drawbridge. They groaned beneath his weight. He ran to the far end of the drawbridge and looked up, his sword at the ready.

Kaymon was on top of the battlements, roaring as she stared down at him.

"Follow me, if you can!" Tom shouted. "Or are you too tired?"

With a ferocious snarl, Kaymon leaped off the castle walls. She plunged down toward the drawbridge, roaring and slavering.

Her tremendous weight landed heavily on the rotten drawbridge. With a crack, the wooden planks collapsed. A long splinter of wood flew through the air toward Tom. He ducked, but the sharp edges of the splinter grazed his cheek, drawing blood.

The massive hound fell into the moat, sending up a torrent of slimy green water. Tom stood at the edge, watching as the evil Beast floundered, gasping and straining to keep her head above the foul waters.

He felt a moment of pity, but it passed. Kaymon was nothing but evil.

Elenna appeared at the gateway. Carefully avoiding the hole in the drawbridge, she ran out to Tom.

The light was fading from the Beast's wicked eyes as the weeds tangled around her body, pulling her down. As the huge head slipped under the thrashing water for the final time, Tom saw the waters begin to spin, as if an invisible stick were stirring the moat water.

Faster and faster the whirlpool spun, and then a hole opened up at its center.

"Look!" cried Elenna, pointing to blue sky and snow-clad mountains that had appeared at the bottom of the hole. "It's Avantia! We'll be able to get Tartok home!"

A sudden fear filled Tom's heart. The gateway to Avantia would stay with them for only a few precious moments.

Where was Tartok?

CHAPTER NINE

SHADOW PLAY

Tom turned at the sound of huge feet beating a path across the moor.

"Tartok!" he shouted in relief, seeing the great, shaggy ice beast racing toward them. Storm was galloping in her wake.

"Here she comes!" Elenna cried. "And she's carrying Silver!"

Tom saw the limp shape of the wolf in Tartok's arms. "She must have understood that it was time to come to us," Tom said.

The good Beast came to a halt and crouched so that Elenna could examine Silver. The wolf was weak but still alive, and he even managed

to lick Elenna's hand as she leaned anxiously over him.

"The wounds are all healed," Elenna said, checking Silver's fur. "But I think he's still exhausted from the ordeal. He can't even stand."

Tartok looked at Tom with her huge, kind eyes and snorted softly.

"She wants to take Silver back to Avantia so he can get well again," Tom said, grateful once more to the ruby in his belt, which allowed him to understand Tartok.

"Yes," Elenna said. "That's a good idea." She threw her arms around Silver's neck. "We'll see you very soon," she said, hiding her face in his thick gray fur.

Tom looked down into the moat. The whirling water was beginning to slow and the gateway was shrinking. Soon it would be gone and Tartok would be trapped here.

"Elenna!" Tom warned gently. "We don't have much time!"

Elenna stepped back. "No, of course," she said, wiping her sleeve across her eyes.

"Tartok!" Tom called. "Jump!"

Still cradling the injured wolf in her arms, the ice beast lumbered to the edge of the moat. She looked over her shoulder, grunting her thanks, then leaped into the gateway.

The water churned as she disappeared; then the spinning waters came to a halt, leaving only slowly spreading ripples.

"I hope he'll be safe," Elenna murmured, staring down into the water.

Tom rested his hand on her shoulder. "I'm sure he will," he said. "Aduro will make him fit and well again in no time. You'll see."

Storm thrust his head between them, nuzzling up against Elenna's face.

"I missed you, boy!" Tom said, stroking the stallion's long nose and patting his neck. "You did well, helping Tartok to look after Silver. But I have another job for you, Storm. You'll have to take us to our next Quest. I'm sure Aduro will soon tell us what it is."

Just then something caught Tom's attention: a bright glint that shone up from the surface of the moat, close to where he had last seen Kaymon.

"What's that?" he asked, walking to the water's edge.

"It's the diamond from Kaymon's collar," Elenna said.

"Yes, it is!" said Tom. "I think I can reach it." He crouched, leaning out over the stagnant water, while Elenna held on to his belt to stop him from falling.

The diamond was just out of reach. He drew his sword and with the point gently edged the jewel toward himself. At last he was able to pick it up. He rubbed it on his tunic, cleaning off the slime.

"Another jewel for my belt!" he said. "I wonder what it will do?"

"Fit it in place and we'll soon find out," Elenna urged him.

Tom set the diamond into his belt.

"Well?" Elenna asked. "Do you feel anything?"

Tom shook his head. "I feel exactly the same," he said.

A few moments passed and Tom was just beginning to wonder if anything would happen at all, when the diamond let out a single blinding pulse of white light.

Tom rubbed his eyes. "What just happened?" he gasped.

He blinked a couple of times to clear his vision, and when he looked at Elenna it was to see her staring openmouthed at something behind his back.

He turned. The high sun cast his shadow at his feet. But something odd was happening — the shadow was moving on its own. Even as Tom stood gazing down at it, the shadow picked itself up out of the grass and stood in front of him with its hands on its hips, its head turning slowly.

"Er . . . hello there . . ." Tom ventured.

The shadow jumped back, as if startled to hear Tom's voice. Then it doubled over, its hands on its knees.

"He's laughing!" Elenna gasped.

The shadow straightened up again and ran lightly toward the moor.

Tom grinned. "Thanks to Kaymon's diamond, I think we have another companion on our Quest!"

The shadow leaped into the air, soundlessly clapping its hands. As he ran ahead, Tom watched, laughing. With their new friend, they'd be more than ready for Malvel's next challenge.

TOM'S QUEST CONTINUES WITH . . .

BEASTQUEST®

THE DARK REALM

⤙ BOOK SEVENTEEN ⤚

TUSK
THE MIGHTY MAMMOTH

A FEROCIOUS BEAST LIKE
NO OTHER!

WILL TOM SUCCEED IN HIS QUEST?
FIND OUT IN . . .

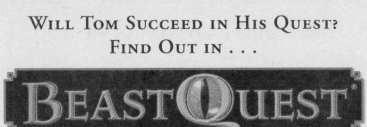

THE DARK REALM

→ BOOK EIGHTEEN ←

STING
THE SCORPION MAN

THE EXCITING CONCLUSION TO THE
DARK REALM SAGA!